Seeing
Double

PUFFIN BOOKS

Published by the Penguin Group
Penguin Books Ltd, 80 Strand, London WC2R 0RL, England
Penguin Group (USA) Inc., 375 Hudson Street, New York, New York 10014, USA
Penguin Group (Canada), 90 Eglinton Avenue, East, Suite 700, Toronto,
Ontario, Canada M4P 2Y3 (a division of Pearson Penguin Canada Inc.)
Penguin Ireland, 25 St Stephen's Green, Dublin 2, Ireland (a division of Penguin Books Ltd)
Penguin Group (Australia), 250 Camberwell Road, Camberwell, Victoria
3124, Australia (a division of Pearson Australia Group Pty Ltd)
Penguin Books India Pvt Ltd, 11 Community Centre, Panchsheel Park, New Delhi – 110 017, India
Penguin Group (NZ), cnr Airborne and Rosedale Roads, Albany, Auckland 1310, New Zealand
(a division of Pearson New Zealand Ltd)
Penguin Books (South Africa) (Pty) Ltd, 24 Sturdee Avenue, Rosebank, Johannesburg 2196,
South Africa

Penguin Books Ltd, Registered Offices: 80 Strand, London WC2R 0RL, England

www.penguin.com

First published in the USA by Grosset & Dunlap, a division of Penguin Young Readers Group 2005
First published in Great Britain in Puffin Books 2005
3

Made and printed in England by Clays Ltd, St Ives plc

British Library Cataloguing in Publication Data
A CIP catalogue record for this book is available from the British Library

ISBN 0–141–32033–8

Seeing
Double

By Christine N. Roberts

PUFFIN

Chapter 1

"Jade!"

Cloe tried to get her friend's attention. The two girls were passing notes during Art Study as their teacher, Mr. Del Rio, was lecturing about European painters. Cloe and Jade were best friends, along with Sasha and Yasmin. Though they were each very different, they did everything together. The four were inseparable.

Art Study was a unique class, combining art history lectures and actual studio time. It was a tough class to get into. You had to have top marks in other art and history classes, and submit a portfolio of work before being admitted.

If she was going to be *the* top fashion designer, Jade would need good marks in this class to get into the best design school. Jade and Cloe were both part of the lucky few who got into the class, which was no surprise—considering how artistic they both were. Jade was always wearing the most cutting-edge fashions, and her friends always thought she was a step ahead of everyone else in the fashion world. Cloe loved fashion, too, and was an amazing artist. No one could draw or paint as well as Cloe did.

"Jade and Cloe!" Mr. Del Rio scolded, interrupting the note-passing fest.

Suddenly, a new girl was standing in the area right in front of Jade and Cloe's desks.

"I'm sure you'll make Nona feel very welcome," Mr. Del Rio said.

Cloe shifted her books over to the other side of the table. "Hi!" she greeted the new girl.

"Hey," she said.

Nona was tall, with a thick mane of brown hair. She was wearing a sparkly red camisole and faded blue jeans with a gold chain as a belt. Her eyes were brown and doe-like, giving her an aura of sweetness. But Jade could see that Nona was feeling a bit uncertain—which was completely understandable for a new student.

"Hi," she said to Nona as the girl sat down. "Welcome to the coolest class at Stiles High!"

At that, Nona brightened. "I know. I heard all about it when I left my old school. I couldn't wait to get here so I could take this class."

"We'll introduce you to the rest of our buds at lunch," Cloe offered.

"That would be great," Nona said. "I don't know anyone here, other than my sister."

"Is she an artist, too?" Cloe asked.

"Sort of," Nona said, then quickly turned to Jade. "I love your necklace!"

"Thanks," Jade said, fingering it. "I picked it out to go with this skirt."

"That's cool," Nona said. "I can't wait to go shopping around here!"

"We've got a great mall here." Cloe assured her. "We'll take you there after school. Come on, we'll walk you out of class and show you around the school a bit."

As soon as they got to the hallway after class, another new student walked up to Nona. "There you are!" she said. "I need to use the cell phone."

Jade eyed the newcomer. She looked exactly like Nona, down to the thick, brown hair and brown eyes—but she dressed so differently that at first, it was difficult to see how much they resembled each other. "Uh, this is my twin sister—" Nona started.

"My name's Tess," the new girl interrupted, tossing a look at Jade and over her shoulder at Cloe. "Hey." She turned back to her sister. "I have to call a friend to pick me up. I'm staying after school to meet with some art committee."

Cloe looked at Tess. She was wearing black

pants with black stitching, a cut-off t-shirt that said "Miss Understood" and a red leather jacket with a funky zipper. Tess definitely had style, but you could tell by her clothes that she was rougher around the edges than her sister.

Nevertheless, Cloe couldn't help but appreciate Tess's originality. "I'm Cloe," she said. "And that's Jade. I heard you're an artist, too," she said.

"This school doesn't appreciate true art," Tess quickly declared.

Nona looked at them, but she didn't say anything. She quickly handed her sister a cell phone, and Tess started dialing.

"Uh," Cloe started. "You're not allowed to use cell phones in school." Tess didn't pay any attention to her. "It's a rule here," Cloe continued. "You have to use the pay phones and only during lunch, so we usually just put notes in each other's lockers when we want to reach each other." But Tess didn't bother to listen. She turned her back on the girls.

Nona looked at her sister's back. "I'll tell her later."

"We'll see you at lunch," Jade said. "You can meet the rest of the gang. I know Sasha and Yasmin are going to love to meet you"

"That would be great!" Nona smiled.

"And I'll also leave a note for Dylan to round up the guys, then we'll all give you the complete lowdown on the coolest high school ever!"

Cloe was excited to introduce her new friend

to everyone. While she and Jade were nearly inseparable from Yasmin and Sasha, they also hung out a lot with their guy friends, Cameron, Dylan, Koby, Cade, and Eitan. Koby and Cade were away at an exchange program for the semester, but Cloe knew that Cameron, Dylan, and Eitan would love to meet Nona. "Great!" Nona said, and linked arms with Cloe. "Let's go! You can show me where math class is."

As Cloe and Nona left, Jade wrote her note to Dylan asking him to meet up at lunch. She finished it just as the bell rang.

"Yikes," she said, trying to stuff the note in Dylan's locker while grabbing her backpack. Then she turned back to say goodbye to Tess, but Tess was still holding the phone to her ear. Jade waved instead, but she didn't think that Tess saw her. *I'll catch up with her at lunch*, Jade thought as she headed down the hall.

Chapter 2

"I have big news," Cloe announced at lunch. Her best friends Sasha and Yasmin turned to face her. "There's a new girl at school!"

"Her name is Nona," Jade added. "We invited her to lunch."

"There she is!" Cloe stood up and waved frantically across the cafeteria.

By the doors, the new girl saw Cloe's wave and moved toward their table. As other kids got out of the way, Yasmin could see she was dressed edgy, but definitely with style.

"Wait a second," said Cloe, as she

instinctively stopped waving. "That's not even her."

Jade craned her neck for a better view. "Wait, maybe it was Tess," she suggested.

Cloe's face brightened. "Oh, right!" She began waving again, but the other girl wasn't in sight anymore. "There are *two* new girls. They're twins! Nona and Tess. I feel terrible, but I still have a hard time telling them apart."

"Hi," said a new voice.

The girls looked up to see Nona, smiling sweetly at them.

"I'm Yasmin," Yasmin introduced herself. "And that's Sasha." She pointed to Sasha's side of the table. "You can sit there. The guys should be along soon."

Nona moved to the chair beside Sasha. She was amazed at how different all the girls looked—yet they were all still fashionable and stylin'. In many ways, their fashions said a lot about their distinctive personalities.

Nona's eyes wandered to Sasha's purse. It was a large white bag with gold studs on the sides, with a cord from Sasha's MP-3 player hanging out over the side. Sasha was a huge music fan and dreamed of working in the music industry one day, so it made sense that she always had some tunes on her.

"Is that your purse?" Nona asked Sasha. It's so cute!"

"I got it last week." Sasha said. "Speaking of cute, I wonder where the guys are?"

"Jade, did you leave them a note?" Yasmin asked.

"Of course," Jade replied. "In Dylan's locker."

"Dylan was late to math," Sasha said. "Maybe he didn't have time to get it."

"But he always hits his locker before lunch," Yasmin pointed out.

Nona looked back and forth between the girls. "Wow. Who else do you all hang out with?"

"Well, there's Dylan," Yasmin added. "He's as into fashion as we are—he says he likes to dress to impress."

"And Eitan," Jade said. "Eitan works at the juice bar in the mall, so we always visit him when we're there."

"And we're there a lot," Cloe said. "Wait! Don't forget about Cameron."

"Of course not, Angel!" Jade said sweetly. The girls all knew Cloe had a crush on Cameron, even if they never admitted it to each other.

" 'Angel' ?" Nona repeated with a puzzled look on her face. "I thought your name was Cloe."

The girls laughed. "We call her Angel because she's always so nice," Yasmin said. "Jade is 'Kool Kat', because she's always wearing something cool and happenin'."

"And Sasha is 'Bunny Boo', the queen of hip-hop," Jade explained.

Sasha bopped her head a bit. "That's me! And Yasmin is 'Pretty Princess'."

"Got it. Wait, what's your nickname again?" Nona asked, pointing to Cloe.

"It's Angel. But the way I treated Tess before . . . I'm not so sure I deserve it anymore," Cloe added sadly.

Nona looked around, concerned. "What happened with Tess?"

"I thought she was you, so I tried to call her over. Then when I saw who she was I stopped! I didn't do it to be mean, though. I just wasn't thinking," Cloe explained.

"People are always mixing us up," Nona said.

"That must be a pain," Yasmin observed.

"Yeah, it bothers Tess a lot, but we deal." Nona shrugged. She brightened again. "So tell me about the mall."

"Look! There's Cameron!" Sasha said, pointing.

They all turned to see Cameron, Dylan and Eitan hustling into the line just as the doors were closing.

"Yuck," Sasha said. "Just in time for dried-out mac."

"That's definitely not like them," Sasha said, "They're usually the first ones in the cafeteria for lunch time. I wonder if everything's okay?"

"Well, we gotta jet to class. So we'll have to find out later," Sasha said. "We should all just get together after school. That's when you can meet them, Nona. I'll leave him a note to gather the other boys and meet up this afternoon."

"Where?" Nona asked eagerly.

The girls looked at one another, then at the new girl. "The mall, of course!"

Chapter 3

Cloe was heading to her locker after lunch when she saw a flash of long brown hair down the hall. "Nona?"

The girl turned. The crowd parted a bit, but from the red leather jacket, Cloe could now see that it was Tess who was turning away. Cloe went after her. "Tess!"

Tess stopped and waited for Cloe.

"Hi, sorry about that," Cloe said as she got closer. "I can't tell you and Nona apart yet!"

Tess shrugged. "I'm used to that."

"I'm sorry I did that at lunch too," Cloe

went on. "I should've invited you over."

"It's okay," Tess said, looking down the hall. "I had other people to sit with."

"We invited Nona to the mall this afternoon. It's got some slammin' stores. You want to come with us?"

"I have that art committee thing."

"Oh, right." Cloe thought for a moment. "Do you want any help? I'm in the class, so—"

"No, thanks," Tess replied, cutting her off. "I have my own style."

"Yes, I know." Cloe pointed down. "Your boots are rockin'!"

"Thanks," Tess said, smiling. "I—"

"Hey, Cloe," a voice interrupted them.

The girls looked up to see a guy bearing

down on them. "Cameron," Cloe said. "This is Tess. She's new—"

"Hi," Cameron said, without letting her finish. "Did you hear about Dylan? I heard he got detention or something."

"Really?" Cloe was shocked.

"Yeah, he was late for class before lunch and the teacher was upset."

"He was late for lunch, too," Cloe remembered. "Maybe his watch is slow or something."

"Watch?" Cameron asked. "Dylan doesn't wear a watch."

"I wonder—" Cloe turned around. "Tess?" Cloe was confused. "She's gone. Did you see her leave?"

"Yeah," Cameron said. "She just walked away."

"Oh," Cloe replied. "I hope she doesn't think I was ignoring her."

"Nah. I wouldn't worry about it, Angel. You don't seem like someone who would do that." Cameron headed off.

Cloe had a study period next, so she headed for the student lounge, pulling out her notebook along the way. She felt terrible that Dylan had detention. She couldn't wait to see him later at the mall that afternoon—then she could find out what was going on.

Later that day at the mall, the girls gathered in the food court, waiting for the guys to show up.

"That's strange. Even Eitan isn't here yet, Yasmin observed, pointing across the juice bar where Eitan worked a part-time job.

"Maybe the boss has him working in the back," Sasha suggested.

"But he'd at least come out to say hi," Cloe said. "And what about the other guys?"

"Maybe they're in the record store?" Sasha said. "The new releases came out today."

"Let's go there!" Nona exclaimed.

Cloe laughed. "Okay, but then straight to the clothing stores."

The girls went to the record store, but

couldn't find the boys anywhere, so they decided to hit the stores until they showed up.

Forty-five minutes later, Cloe was paying for clothes inside Clothes 'N' Counters.

"Still no guys," Sasha observed, looking over the railing down toward the food court. She and Cloe were waiting for Jade, Yasmin, and Nona at their designated meeting place. "What's with them today?"

Just then Jade and Yasmin arrived, escorting Nona and her shopping bags.

"What did you get?" Cloe asked.

"A few tops that Jade said would look good on me, some necklaces, and the most stylin' pair of pants you've ever seen!"

"Wow!" Sasha said. "You scored!"

"Well," Nona said, "Jade helped a lot. And Yasmin, too. I just wish I had black boots that matched it," Sasha laughed.

"Wait, your sister was wearing some today. Can't you just borrow those? Cloe asked.

Nona's face fell a bit. "She doesn't want to lend them to me."

"That's because we don't have the same style, Nona," a new voice said. The girls all turned to see Tess.

Nona didn't say anything, so Cloe jumped in. She didn't like how Tess was treating Nona, but figured it was just sister drama.

"Hi, Tess, I'm glad you came . . ."

"How'd your meeting go?" Jade jumped in.

Tess's face fell a bit. "They didn't take me.

No offense Cloe, I know you're in this class and all, but I don't think they would recognize real art if it landed on their desks."

Yasmin had to hold herself back from leaping to Cloe's defense. Everyone knew that Cloe was a great artist with a bright future.

Tess pointed at Nona's bag. "You bought something already?"

"Yes," Nona said, "really cute pan—"

Tess eyed her sister. "You have five minutes to finish up. Then I'm leaving. Meet me by the fountain." She walked away.

The girls were silent for a moment. "I'm sorry about that," Nona said. "Tess has a strong personality, but she is hardly ever rude. She must be very disappointed about the class. She's so passionate about art, it must be upsetting that the school doesn't recognize her style."

"It's okay," Cloe reassured Nona.

"What kind of art does she do?" Yasmin asked. "Collages," Nona said, brightening again. "They're really cool, but they're not everybody's taste."

"Maybe she just hasn't found the right audience," Yasmin said gently.

"Maybe," Nona said slowly. "I guess I'd better go, if I want to get a ride back with her."

"Relax," Cloe said. "We'll take you home."

Sasha slipped her arm through Nona's. "Now let's hit Maxie's, the store with the great bags. Then we'll go see what's keeping those boys."

Nona smiled happily to herself. She had

been really worried about moving to a new school, but now it looked like she was going to fit in just fine.

Chapter 4

The next day at school, Cloe came to Cameron's locker, determined to find out what happened to the boys the day before. She was going to be late for art class, but she absolutely needed to know they hadn't shown up at the mall yesterday. Just then, she saw Nona heading toward her.

"Nona, can you please do me the hugest favor?" Cloe asked. "I'm going to be late for class— could you put this note in Cameron's locker for me? It's locker number 812, right near our history classroom."

"Of course," Nona said, turning away.

Just then, Cloe remembered she wanted Nona to meet up with her later that day. She turned around and saw a girl with long, brown hair walking with her back toward her. She was about to yell out Nona's name when she caught herself. There was that red leather jacket again. It was Tess she was looking at. Nona must have already turned the corner.

"Hey, Tess, hi!" Cloe said with a bright smile. Even though Tess had been stand-offish, Cloe was determined to be nice to her. "How are you doing?"

"Not so great," Tess said. "You guys could have told me you were giving Nona a ride home with you yesterday. I ended up waiting for her for an hour."

"Oh my God!" Cloe gasped. "We totally forgot. I really am so sorry you had to keep on waiting."

"Whatever," Tess said, shrugging her shoulders. She was about to leave when Cloe interrupted her.

"Wait," Cloe said. "Did you see the sign-up sheet for the literary magazine?"

"Why would I care about that?" Tess sounded very impatient.

"Because," Cloe explained, "they're always looking for new illustrators, and I hear you're an amazing artist."

"I do collage, not illustration," Tess said abruptly as she tossed her hair over her shoulder and walked away.

Cloe felt bad. She knew that Nona did collages. She just forgot. And now she insulted her when all she was trying to do was make her feel included.

"So what's the deal?" Cloe asked later that night. She was on a conference call with the rest of the girls, trying to figure out what was going on with the guys. Cameron never showed up that day after she had asked Nona to put the note in his locker.

"I don't know," Cloe said. "They have never just not shown up somewhere like that. It's not like them. And afterwards, I was really clear in my note to Cameron that he should meet us in the quad."

"And you put it in his locker?" Yasmin asked.

"Well, I gave it to Nona to put in his locker, 'cuz I was running late for class. She was in that wing, anyway."

"Did you give Nona the right number?" Jade asked.

"Of course."

Cloe began flipping through her notebook, looking for the page where she'd jotted down everyone's schedule.

"Did you try calling one of them?" Jade asked of no one in particular.

"Yes," Yasmin said.

"There's no answer at Dylan's, and Cameron's went to voice mail."

"That's weird," Cloe said. "He never turns it off, except in class."

"Or the movies," Yasmin reminded her.

"What about Dylan?" Jade asked.

"Well, Eitan's working, or should be," Cloe said. Cloe could hear Yasmin tapping her pen. "You got an idea, Pretty Princess?"

"Well, the only way we're going to figure this out is to get the guys all in one place."

The other girls laughed.

"Right," Cloe teased, "because that's been so easy to do this week!"

Chapter 5

"I heard your friend got detention," Nona announced in Art Study the next day as she slipped into the seat between Cloe and Jade.

"Which friend?" Jade asked.

"Um," Nona thought. "I think it was Eitan. I'm not sure, though, 'cause you know, I haven't actual met any of them yet."

"Do you know why?" Cloe asked.

"He was late for bio," Nona said as she put her bag on the floor.

Cloe and Jade exchanged a look. "That's like a double whammy for him," Cloe whispered as Mr. Del Rio turned on the slide projector and a student near the door flipped off the lights. "He's supposed to work today, right after school."

"I know," Jade said. "If he's late, he could lose his job!"

After her music class, Cloe finally had the opportunity to corner Cameron. "Cameron!" she called out when she saw him.

To her surprise, he didn't look happy to see her. That bothered her, but she was going to find out what was going on.

"Oh, hey," Cameron said.

"Where have you all been? We've been leaving notes—"

"Yeah, we've been getting your notes!"

"What's that supposed to mean?" she asked.

"Your notes: 'Meet in the main lobby after school.' 'Meet us in the caf before Study.' And yesterday, 'Meet us at the baseball diamond'? Eitan almost lost his job because of that little stunt."

Cloe was floored. "The main lobby? The cafeteria? And since when do we ever meet at the baseball diamond?"

Cameron shrugged. "I don't know, I just followed the notes."

Cloe shook her head. "That doesn't make any sense. That's not what we said."

Cameron's face seemed to soften a bit. "Okay, maybe it was just a mistake. But I gotta go." He turned away, then came back. "You might want to avoid Eitan for a few days. He got detention following what those notes had to say."

"I know," Cloe said sadly, "Nona told me."

"That new girl?" Cameron asked in a harsh tone.

"Yes, Nona," Cloe shot back. "What's your problem with her? You two haven't even met yet!"

"Yes, I have," he said. "In history class. She's always saying rude things about you guys."

"What?" Cloe felt woozy. How could Nona do this to her?

"I gotta go. I don't want to be late." Cameron shouldered his pack.

Cloe's mind was awhirl.

"Hey," Cameron said. His face was full of concern now. "I didn't mean to be so harsh. Maybe she just made the wrong first impression."

"Maybe..." Cloe didn't know what to think. "Hey, we'll make a plan. We'll all get together— somewhere new and fun—and you'll see how cool and sweet she is."

Cameron didn't look convinced, but he said, "Right, Angel, I'm sure she is." He headed off and Cloe went in search of her friends.

"Things are worse than we thought," Cloe said when she up with Jade and Sasha between classes.

Jade felt her stomach drop. "How could they be any worse than they are already? The boys have been ignoring all our notes. It seems like they don't want to hang out any more. What's worse than that?

"Well, Cameron just told me they've been getting notes that tell them to go to the wrong places," Cloe said.

"How is that possible?" Yasmin asked.

"I don't know," Cloe said sounding hurt and confused. "But that's not all. He also told me that he's overheard Nona talking about us behind our backs."

That statement got a collective gasp from Sasha, Jade, and Yasmin.

"It's crazy," Cloe said. "It seemed like we were all hitting it off so well."

"And now it seems like we're not getting along with anybody," Sasha said, glumly.

Chapter 6

"Dylan wasn't home, then his line was busy all night," Yasmin reported in home room the next day. The girls had decided to try and talk to the boys rather than leave notes this time.

"Eitan was working the closing shift at the juice bar," Yasmin reported. "I didn't want to call too late."

Yasmin tapped her lip with a bright pink fingernail. "What about Cameron? Did anybody talk to him?"

"I will!" Cloe lit up. The other three girls exchanged knowing glances, as if on cue.

Somehow, no one was surprised that Cloe was the first to volunteer to speak to Cameron.

Planting herself in front of Cameron's locker, Cloe stayed put until the next bell.

"Cloe?"

She turned as quickly as her platform boots would let her and came face-to-face with Cameron. "There you are!"

"Hey," he replied, a bit sullenly. "Long time no see."

"It seems like we can never connect anymore!" she said with a laugh.

"I know!" Cameron said angrily. "Why have you guys been treating us this way?"

"Wh-what are you talking about? You guys are the ones who are always blowing us off!"

"Oh right—like we'd ever invite you to the movies and then not show."

"When did that happen?"

Cameron looked like he didn't believe her. "Two days ago. Sasha left me a note saying we should all meet up and catch a movie." He stuffed his hands in the pockets of his cargo pants.

"That's a good idea," Cloe said. "We could use a chance to—"

"You don't get it." Cameron shook his head. "The note was for *that* day. A movie *that day*."

"Two days ago? But we never planned—"

"When I ran into you in the hall, you said you'd make a plan for somewhere fun. Then I got the note from Sasha to meet at the movies that afternoon. You were bringing a new friend and all. So we went."

"You did?"

"Yes, all of us." Cameron emphasized. "And we all bought tickets. *And* popcorn. And for your new friend as well!"

"Oh, no! That's when your cell phones were off!" Cloe realized. "We couldn't reach you."

Cameron looked hopeful. "You tried to call us to tell us you couldn't make it? I knew—

"No," Cloe interrupted. "I mean, we weren't *at* the movies. We were ...where we'd said we'd be."

"What?" Cameron sounded angry again. He began twirling the combination on his locker. "I wish you would make up your mind. First the soccer field, then the yearbook office, then the movies ..." Cameron reached into his locker. He pushed aside some books and pulled out a few pieces of torn notebook paper. He handed them to Cloe. "We're getting tired of always showing when nobody's there."

She looked down at the note in her hand:

Cameron, meet us on the soccer field before lunch. We have a new friend to introduce to you guys.

To Cloe's shock, the note was signed. By her.

"Uh, Cameron, I didn't write this note."

"What?" He looked confused. "Of course you did." He grabbed it back from her and read it again. "It has your name ..." Cameron trailed off and Cloe knew he was thinking of all the other notes they had exchanged. The handwriting wasn't even close.

"But why would someone sign your name?" He wondered.

"I don't know," Cloe said. "But we're going to get to the bottom of this!"

Following a few phone calls, the girls were gathered in Quick Clicks, an Internet café near school.

Cloe was practically blowing steam out of her ears. "You guys won't believe this!" she announced.

"What is it, Angel?" Sasha asked.

Cloe pulled a handful of notes from her bag. "Look at these!" she said, tossing them on the table. "I got them from the guys."

The girls each lifted one from the pile and

read it. "So?" Sasha asked. "They're notes."

Jade was going through each one. "They're from us. So what?"

"Look closer," Cloe ordered.

Jade sighed and began sorting the notes into little piles. "This one is from Sasha, and this one is from me . . ." Jade blinked and looked at the note again. "No, it's not."

"Right!" Cloe crowed. "These notes are not from us."

"Sure they are, Angel," Sasha said, pulling a few pieces of paper over to her. "They—"

Yasmin grabbed the note nearest to her. "It says, 'Meet us on the soccer field.' "

Then Cloe leaned over to get a closer look at the note. "And it's signed, 'Cloe,'" but it's not my handwriting!"

Sasha snatched up another note. "This isn't from me."

"I know," Cloe said. "None of them are. I tracked down as many of the guys as I could find, and got any notes they had on them."

She fished around under the table and produced her backpack again. "I have others that seemed real to me. But these"—she nodded at the tabletop—"are the ones that looked off."

"Angel, what do you mean?" Sasha asked.

"All the fake notes have one thing in common."

"What's that?" Jade asked, puzzled.

Cloe didn't look happy to be answering this question. "They all refer to Nona."

Chapter 7

"The guys aren't thinking straight," Jade said. "Otherwise they might've caught that."

"Or at least have noticed it wasn't our handwriting!" Sasha said indignantly.

"Okay," Yasmin said, "let's be fair. It's not like we usually read the notes so carefully, either. We just read the note and trash it."

"So what do we do now?" Cloe asked.

"And what about Nona?" Sasha asked.

"What about me?"

The girls looked up. Nona was standing beside their table, a chai grande in her hand.

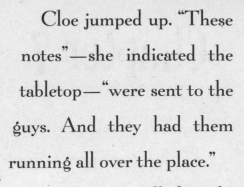

Cloe jumped up. "These notes"—she indicated the tabletop—"were sent to the guys. And they had them running all over the place."

"They are all forged," Sasha said. Yet every single one mentions getting to meet you."

"You ..." Nona stammered, "think I forged notes? Why would I do a thing like that?"

Cloe reached out an embracing arm, but Nona shook her off. "You guys are crazy," Nona announced. "And mean. Tess was right about you all."

And then she stormed off.

"I feel terrible. I definitely could've handled that better," Cloe said.

"We all could've," Jade agreed.

"Well, if she didn't have a problem with us before, she certainly does now." Cloe said.

"And we're not any closer to figuring out who's behind those crazy notes." Yasmin added.

The girls were quiet for a moment. It was Sasha who finally broke the silence. "Now what do we do?"

Chapter 8

"Is that Nona or Tess?" Sasha asked at lunch the next day. The girls turned to look at the other table. A girl with dark brown hair and light brown eyes was sitting down. She was wearing the white pants that Nona bought at the mall, and Tess's signature red leather jacket.

"I hope it's Nona so I can apologize to her about yesterday," Cloe said.

"Either way, they must have made up, because they seem to be sharing clothes," Yasmin said.

Cloe craned her neck for a better look at

Tess/Nona's table. "Maybe we can tell by seeing who else is sitting at her table." The other girls followed Cloe's lead. What they saw was a table of kids dressed in black boots and leather jackets. "Tess," they said in unison.

"So where's Nona?" Cloe asked.

"I haven't seen her," Jade said, and the other girls realized they hadn't, either.

"Makes you wonder," Sasha began, "What Nona meant when she said Tess was right about us."

Cloe made a small face. "I guess we haven't really impressed Tess."

The warning bell rang, and the girls cleaned up their garbage and bussed their trays.

Cloe realized she left her metallic notebook

at the table. When she went back to get it, there was a tap on her shoulder. "Te- Nona?" Cloe asked, surprised.

"Yup. Nona." The girl nodded. "You knew it was me, right?"

"Um...well...to be honest," Cloe hesitated, "the jacket threw me off."

Nona gave a knowing chuckle. "It's confusing, I know. Sometimes, Tess and I share clothes. We used to do it all the time in our old school, but then Tess decided that we should stop. Now I just wear her stuff once in a while."

"I guess once I know you better, it'll be easier to tell you apart," Cloe said, looking down at her feet.

Nona nodded in agreement.

"Anyway," Cloe continued, I'm glad you came by because I wanted to apologize for yesterday. I should have—"

"It's okay," Nona interrupted. "Don't worry about it. That's why I came over here. I wanted to apologize too. I totally overreacted."

Suddenly the crowd was moving along again, and Cloe was getting pushed away from Nona. "So we're good?" Cloe shouted.

"We're good!" Nona shouted back as she was carried off into the shuffle.

Cloe was still standing in the hallway thinking about how friendly Nona had just been and how difficult it was to imagine her trash-talkin' the girls the way Cameron said, when an idea occurred to her. If Nona could be mistaken for Tess, couldn't Tess be mistaken for Nona?

Cloe detoured to the art room and slipped into the back of the class. She grabbed a few sheets of colored paper off a shelf and bolted back out to the hallway. Leaning up against a locker, she dashed off a quick note.

"Y," she wrote, "Nona and Tess switch clothes some times. Does this mean anything?"

Cloe headed for Yasmin's locker. For the first time since this whole mess began, she had an idea of who might be behind the forged notes. And maybe, just maybe if everyone pitched in, they'd find that person before any more damage was done.

Chapter 9

Looks like we're headed to the mall again!
Cloe thought happily.

The boys arrived at the mall with a few
notes—some old, some new, which they spread
out on a table at the food court.

The guys were still mad. But at least they
knew once and for all that their friends were not
to blame.

"I don't get it," Cameron said for the
umpteenth time. "Who would do this?"

"Yeah, man," Dylan said, crossing his arms.
"Who would wreck our schedules?"

"And school records," Eitan added. He was leaning over the table, one booted foot propped on a chair rung. He kept an eye on the juice bar.

Jade shook her head. "We feel terrible that this happened."

"But it's not our fault," Sasha added.

"We know," Cameron said, looking around at his friends. "We know that now."

"Not that we thought you guys were being mean on purpose or anything," Eitan added.

"We know," Yasmin said.

"It takes all kinds." Dylan shook his head.

Eitan checked his watch. "So, we cool?"

Sasha rolled her eyes and Jade shook her head. "No, Eitan, we're not. We still have to figure out why this happened and who's behind it."

The guys looked confused. "Why?" Dylan asked. "It's over."

"Is it?" Yasmin asked.

"We didn't get any other notes today," Eitan pointed out. "Just yours."

"Right, so . . ." Cameron said, standing. "As long as we use the different paper we're cool."

Dylan reached for his backpack. "Want to go check out CDs?"

Cameron left with Dylan, but Eitan headed back to work.

The guys were clearly over it.

"We'll catch up with you at Spinners," Jade said, ignoring the looks from the other girls.

"Later!" Cameron flashed them a wave.

"So now what?" Cloe asked. "I still want to catch the person who is signing our names and give them a piece of my mind!"

"Me too!" Sasha chimed in.

Yasmin opened her notebook. "Cloe told me something about Nona and Tess switching outfits and here's what I came up with . . ."

Chapter 10

The next day Yasmin decided to find Eitan and see if he found any CDs at Spinners.

As she leaned against Eitan's row of lockers waiting for him to show up, she heard a familiar voice. "Hey." Yasmin turned. Nona was standing there, staring at her.

"Nona?" Yasmin asked, remembering what Cloe had told them all yesterday about the sisters switching clothes. Yasmin had to admit she hadn't looked at each sister too carefully.

"Yes," Nona replied. She looked around. "What are you doing here?"

"I'm waiting for my friend Eitan."

Nona's face fell a bit. "Oh, okay." She pointed behind Yasmin. "That's my locker, though."

"Sorry," Yasmin said, pulling away from it. She watched as Nona spun her combination. And stopped. At first Yasmin thought Nona wanted to hide the combo from Yasmin. Then she realized Nona had misdialed and had to try again.

"It's tough at first," Yasmin said, trying to be friendly. "I always forgot mine."

"I know," Nona agreed. "And I have two to remember."

"Why two?"

"Well, Tess's is downstairs. So we always make sure we know both, in case we're closer to the other one and need a place to stash things."

Nona finally got the door open. The inside of the locker door was decorated with photos of collages. "Wow," she said. "Those are cool."

Nona paused in exchanging her textbooks. She looked at the cards. "Yes. Those are Tess's."

"So this one is her locker?" Yasmin asked.

"No, but those are her pieces. She drew them for me."

Yasmin was floored. The collages were absolutely beautiful. But she didn't really have time to think about that now. What really interested her was the fact that the sisters shared lockers. "Nona," she said slowly. "Where did you say Tess's locker is?"

"Downstairs," Nona replied, with a puzzled expression.

"Downstairs by Dylan's locker?" Yasmin asked.

Nona giggled. "I wouldn't know. I still haven't met him. Remember?

"Oh right," Yasmin said. "Well, is her locker outside the history department?" Yasmin inquired.

"Yes, that's right." Nona closed her locker. "How did you know?"

"Just a guess," Yasmin said slowly, thinking everything through. "Hey Nona, can you meet me after lunch?"

Nona nodded, still backing up. "Where?"

"Outside the gym. By the trophy case."

"I think I've seen it. Okay, later!"

Yasmin watched Nona depart.

She hoped she was on to something. She would catch up with her friends first. Then maybe Cloe would be able to convince Nona to cooperate with them.

Chapter 11

Monday began like any other day. Cloe and Jade were back in Art Study. Just as class started, Nona slipped into the room and headed for the back, where Cloe and Jade were seated.

"Nona!" Mr. Del Rio spoke sharply. "I know that you're new, but I would appreciate it if you were on time for class."

Nona blushed up to her hairline. "I'm so sorry. I thought ... I was supposed to be in the gym."

A few students in class laughed. Cloe and Jade exchanged a look.

Mr. Del Rio merely nodded and let Nona

sit down. The three girls tapped a silent high five before turning their attention to the class.

By the time lunch period rolled around, the entire school was buzzing about Nona. How she'd been late to every class. And she was always claiming she thought she was supposed to be somewhere else.

Because she was new, each teacher had let her off the hook with just a warning.

"Thank goodness the teachers aren't comparing notes," Nona had whispered to Cloe during a between-class lip gloss touch-up.

"Thank goodness we did," Cloe whispered back.

As arranged, Nona didn't appear in the lunchroom during that period. Sasha, Jade,

Yasmin, and Cloe all acted like nothing was wrong. They ate their lunches, swapped food, and talked about their latest mall purchases

At one point Cloe looked up to see Tess, standing beside their table.

"Hi, Tess!" she said brightly. "Want a seat?"

"Have you seen my sister?" Tess asked, looking concerned. She stared off into the distance for a minute. "I've heard . . . some things."

Just then two girls passed by and waved at Tess. She seemed torn between going off with them and confiding in the girls at the table.

The bell rang.

"I need to go!" Tess announced and fled.

After lunch the girls made their way to the auditorium for a presentation on an upcoming field trip.

Halfway through the presentation, the back doors opened and Nona hurried in. Her boots squeaked as she headed down the aisle. The principal addressed her from the stage.

"Miss, are you aware we began this presentation fifteen minutes ago?"

All eyes were trained on Nona. Cloe felt so bad for her. But Nona had been game to help them out, and she knew this would happen.

"Yes, sir. I mean I knew the presentation was now." She held up a piece of notebook paper. "But I got this note to go to the yearbook room and—"

"I can see from here that that isn't an official note from the office," Mr. McNichols said sternly. "In the future, I suggest you pay attention to the difference."

Cloe knew every single kid in the room was thinking about what they'd heard all morning: Nona had been running all over, late everywhere. She hoped Tess had heard it too.

"Yes . . . yes, sir," Nona said, slipping into the seat next to Cloe. Below the principal's sight line, they linked hands.

The presentation continued.

When the bell rang to signal the end of the period, Nona bolted from the auditorium.

The girls looked at each other. This was it.

As planned, Nona slowed her flight long enough for everyone leaving the auditorium to see her enter the quad and sit at one of the picnic tables with a look of misery in her face.

Cloc watched the scene with her friends, standing off to one side, with her fingers crossed.

"Look," Yasmin nudged her. Out in the quad, someone was approaching Nona.

"Let's go," Jade said, opening the door and leading the way outside.

The girls gathered around the table where Nona was sitting at the exact moment Nona looked up at Tess.

"Hi, sis," Nona said. "I guess you saw what happened?"

Tess sat down next to her sister. "Yeah."

"I don't understand," Nona said. "All day long, kids have been handing me notes about changed classrooms. I just thought it was a normal thing at this school. Like maybe when one teacher's absent it threw off the whole day's schedule or something. But now I see someone must have been messing with me. I just don't get why someone would do that?"

"Yes, Tess," Yasmin said, stepping up behind Nona. "Why *would* someone pass fake notes?"

Tess looked around as Jade, Sasha, and Cloe came closer as well. She sighed and looked down. It was obvious she knew she was busted. "Because ... because you didn't like me."

Nona's face turned bright red. "I don't get it," she shouted. "Why would you do this? Why would you send fake notes to my friends? Why would you even care about my friends? You're the one who wanted us to do things separately."

"What?" Jade said.

Tess nodded. "It's true. At our old school, people confused us all the time. Since we both like art, we took a lot of the same classes."

"Before we started here," Nona added, "Tess thought we should try to be more independent."

Tess's eyes began to tear as she turned toward her sister. "I thought that's what I wanted. But then it seemed like everything was going better for you than it was for me and I guess I got jealous."

"Jealous?" Nona asked looking very perplexed. "Jealous of me?"

"Yes, jealous of you. For one thing, you got into the Art Study class and I didn't," Tess said. "So I was afraid that maybe your art was better than mine."

"Oh Tess," Nona said, "Your art is so

amazing! You know that."

"I still don't understand what this has to do with us," Sasha said, with her hands on her hips.

Tess looked embarrassed. "Well, I guess I just felt like you chose Nona over me."

"We didn't choose anyone," Jade corrected her. "We always invited you to join us."

"Right," Cloe said. "You weren't interested."

"You were so into introducing Nona to your other friends," Tess countered. "I got sick of hearing about all the notes."

Yasmin wanted to hear the whole thing.

"When I realized my locker was next to one of the guys', and Nona's was in the same row as another guy's, it was easy to take the notes out of the cracks and replace them with my own."

"Why would you do that?" Sasha asked.

"To get you to ditch Nona," Tess admitted. "I was hoping you'd figure out someone was playing around with the notes and that you'd blame her. I figured if I didn't make the cut, then neither should she."

Nona looked really hurt. "I can't believe you would hurt me and my friends this way. I don't even know what to say to you, Tess."

"I really am very sorry. I never wanted anyone to get into trouble"

"But you did," Yasmin said. "And once you saw that happening, you kept doing it."

"And correct me if I'm wrong, but you also talked trash about us in front of the guys while you were dressed as Nona so that they wouldn't like her either," Cloe said.

Tess nodded. She had no defense. "It's true. It was an awful thing to do. Every time I'd think you'd been nice to me, something would happen that would make me not trust you again. You wouldn't wave me over at lunch. You'd forget what kind of art I do. You'd run off to talk to someone else."

Cloe sat down beside Tess. "I'm sorry we gave you that impression. We never wanted you to feel that way."

"I'm sorry. I'll talk to the main office and make sure the guys don't get permanent marks."

The girls were silent, waiting for her to offer more.

"And I'll also apologize to the guys." Tess said.

There was more silence as everyone tried

to think of what the next step was.

"I like your art," Yasmin said.

Tess practically glowed. "You do? Most people don't get it."

"That's not a bad thing," Yasmin said. "It just means that it's not as simple to understand. You have to think about it more. You know, a little more experimental. But that's a good thing."

Tess was so happy. She looked from the girls to her sister and back. "It's nice to hear that." Her face fell a bit. "Even if I didn't make the class."

"It's only one person's opinion," Yasmin began. "Lots of great artists had to face rejection before their work was accepted."

"Maybe Mr. Del Rio's rejection is a sign that you're going to be famous," Nona said, hugging her sister tight.

The sisters laughed.

Jade could see that up close, they were really quite different. And yet still sisters.

Sasha jumped and stretched. "I'm so glad this is solved. What say we celebrate after school?"

"All of us?" Cloe asked with a smile.

"Of course," Jade said, squeezing Tess's arm. "And I know just what we should do!"

"What?" Tess asked.

"Shopping!" the other girls replied at once.

They laughed.

"Perfect." Yasmin said. "Let me just leave Eitan a note . . ."